ZEBRA
ON THE
GO

For Kyle, Connor, and Kaitlyn, who fill my life with joy
—J. N.

For Karl and Fiona
—L. R.

Ω

Published by
PEACHTREE PUBLISHERS
1700 Chattahoochee Avenue
Atlanta, Georgia 30318-2112
www.peachtree-online.com

Text ©2017 Jill Nogales
Illustrations ©2017 Lorraine Rocha

Edited by Stephanie Fretwell-Hill and Kathy Landwehr
Design and composition by Loraine Joyner and Nicola Carmack
The illustrations were rendered in watercolor and gouache.

Printed in October 2016 by Tien Wah Press in Malaysia
10 9 8 7 6 5 4 3 2 1
First Edition
ISBN 978-1-56145-911-7

Library of Congress Cataloging-in-Publication Data

Names: Nogales, Jill, author. | Rocha, Lorraine, illustrator.
Title: Zebra on the go / by Jill Nogales ; illustrated by Lorraine Rocha.
Description: Atlanta, GA : Peachtree Publishers, [2017] | Summary: When Zebra accidentally steps on Lion's toe, Lion gets angry and begins chasing Zebra in what turns out to be a remarkable show.
Identifiers: LCCN 2015041081
Subjects: | CYAC: Stories in rhyme. | Circus—Fiction. | Zebras—Fiction. | Lion—Fiction. | Adventure and adventurers—Fiction.
Classification: LCC PZ8.3.N727 Zeb 2016 | DDC [E]—dc23 LC record available at *https://lccn.loc.gov/2015041081*

ZEBRA ON THE GO

JILL NOGALES

Illustrated by Lorraine Rocha

PEACHTREE
ATLANTA

Trumpets tooting, cannon shooting.

Music playing, horses neighing.

Flags are flapping, children clapping.

Ready for the show!

Ponies prancing, bear cubs dancing.

Clowns are rushing, trainers brushing.

Cameras flashing, Zebra dashing.

Steps on Lion's toe!

Lion roaring, temper soaring.

Zebra darting, crowd is parting.

Away he's racing, Lion's chasing.

Zebra on the go!

Policeman shouting,
traffic routing.

Teeth are gnashing,
cars are crashing.

Jaws are dropping, hooves are clopping.

Where will Zebra go?

Lion's nearing, Zebra's fearing.

Legs are pumping, heart is thumping.

Children riding, Zebra hiding.

Will Lion ever know?

Lion stalking, vendors gawking.

Zebra peeking, nannies shrieking.

Lion pouncing,
popcorn bouncing.
Zebra on the go!

Sand is flying,
seagulls crying.

Boats are docking,
pier is rocking.

Skipper calling,
sailors falling.

Captain yelling, "Whoa!"

Away they're zooming,
boats are vrooming.

Lion crashing,

water splashing.

Lion sinking.

Fifi

Zebra thinking.

Lion needs a tow!

Fish are darting,
rescue starting.

Ropes are tugging,
motor chugging.

Paws are gripping,
mane is dripping.

Zebra saves his foe!

Chase is ending, friendship mending.

Lion hugging, Zebra shrugging.

Boat horns tooting, sailors hooting.

Cheering, "What a show!"